I0838392

One Night Stand

One Night Stand

One Night Stand

One Night Stand

One Night Stand

© Copyright 2022 Kathryn Reign

All rights reserved. No part of this publication may be reproduced, distributed, or transmitted in any form or by any means, including photocopying, recording, or other electronic or mechanical methods, without the prior written permission of the publisher, except in the case of brief quotations embodied in critical reviews and certain other non-commercial uses permitted by copyright law.

Any references to historical events, real people, or real places are used fictitiously. Names, characters, and places are products of the author's imagination.

Cover Design by Temptation Creations (Quirah Casey)

One Night Stand

Table of Contents

One Night Stand

Prologue

SOCIAL MEDIA IS A GREAT WAY to stay in touch with friends, family, and fans. We see it as a way of life, our main source of connection, and for some of us, our income revenue. Every day, we strive to not only upload and stream content of our own, but we also keep in touch with those we admire, those who admire us, and even those we hate.

We film ourselves doing things people do every day, such as shop, eat, and work out, hyping up these simple and ordinary activities as things people should pay attention to and congratulate us for. We even go as far as to film our homes, every room, every door, every crevice, until there's no privacy left in our lives anymore, our entire existence on display for the world to see. It's become our way of life, our addiction, and most of us don't know to get out until it's too late.

But what happens when social media becomes deadly? What happens when dangerous people see the privacy of our lives online and do more than just watch us and relish in our luxuries and pride? What happens when the very fabric of our lives become exposed to people who want to take advantage of us?

That's exactly what happened to Tara Bardot, a rising social media influencer who only wanted the world to like her, who wanted to share every part of her life with her fans and become completely transparent. And while many of her followers relished in her success and enjoyed the honestly she shared with them, others turned dark, becoming so overly obsessed with her that they don't know how to unleash it in a healthy manner, seeing her as an attainable object that they must have or no one can. Seeing her as someone who belonged to them.

This is the story of Tara Bardot, a young woman fighting for her life.

Chapter One
TARA

"AND… THAT'S A WRAP FOR TODAY! Thank you all so much for joining me today and for subscribing to my channel. Your support truly means the world to me, and I wouldn't be here today without you. I love you all, and I'll see you back here tomorrow at seven! Remember, I'm here every day, and you guys are my life! Bye!!"

Tara Bardot turned off her stream and stepped away from her camera. It was getting late, and she was supposed to meet up with her husband, Rowan, in midtown to celebrate their six years together as husband and wife. He had to work late tonight, telling Tara he'd meet her there instead so he wouldn't have to rush home first to change. And besides, 7pm was usually her time in the evenings. It'll only disturb her if he came in while she was online.

Stripping off her online persona, she hopped into the shower and turned on the water. The steam filling up the bathroom was just what she needed to end her day. As water soaked through her dark blonde hair, she looked over at the mosaic owl sitting on her marble sink. It made her reminisce on her last video, just two days ago, when she gave her fans a tour of her bathroom. From the hand-stitched towels to the gold-framed mirror, all made possible because of her loyal followers, and she couldn't ask for a better life. Her life just seemed so perfect.

As she washed the shampoo off her hair, she wondered what present Rowan had in store for her tonight. He usually went all out with their anniversaries, surprising her each year with a more lavish gift than the last. Last year, he got her a diamond necklace that was worth more than most people's cars. And she was just so ecstatic that the first thing she did was show it off online. She had to share with the world the joys of her life. Otherwise, she didn't see the point in experiencing any of it.

A few minutes later, she turned off the showerhead and walked into her closet to get dressed… but not without some help. She grabbed her phone and turned her camera live, grabbing five different dresses she was debating between and holding each one up to her body while the votes poured in.

"Emerald green it is, thanks guys!"

Then her phone rang. She picked it up, and Rowan was on the other line.

"Hey, babe, I'm getting ready now. I should be there in about forty minutes." Her voice was cheerful and upbeat, like she didn't have a worry in the world.

However, the same couldn't be said for her husband. "For… forty minutes? You were supposed to be here thirty minutes ago! I made reservations, remember? Everything's getting cold!"

"Relax, babe," she said again. "Just order another glass of scotch or something. I'll be there soon.

Besides, you know I can't leave the house unless I'm absolutely perfect."

"Whatever, just hurry the fuck up."

Then he hung up, without even saying goodbye. If Tara didn't know any better, she could swear he was rolling his eyes at her before he hung up.

Typical Rowan, she thought. *Always in such a rush. He just doesn't understand how important my lifestyle is to me. Without it, I'm no one.*

She finished dabbing on the rest of her makeup and pinned a pair of diamond earrings onto her lobes before tucking her petite feet into her heels and heading out the door. The sound and smell of the Big Apple never seemed to stop amazing her. She grew up in the small countryside of Wisconsin, so when she moved to the bustling city that never sleeps, she just couldn't get enough. From the quirky people to the delicious food to the never-ending shopping and Broadway shows, there was always something waiting for her outside her door.

"Hey, Tara, over here! Over here!"

She whipped her head around and saw a young girl running in her direction. She was wearing a pink tutu, with her hair in pigtails, and a face full of makeup. Her glittery pink backpack tossed from side to side as she ran. Her mother wasn't far behind her as she pounced over.

"Tara! Tara Bardot! I can't believe it's you! You're my idol. I LOVE your channel!"

"Aw, that's so sweet. Always a pleasure to meet my fans."

The girl reached into her backpack and pulled out her phone. "Can I get a picture with you, please? My friends will never believe that I met *the* Tara Bardot!"

Tara smiled. "Of course, um…"

"Jessica. Jessica Simmons. And that's my mom!" She pointed behind her as Tara waved.

Six snaps of a camera later, Tara made a quick stop at one of her favorite local coffee shops to grab herself a sugary treat before heading toward the subway. The restaurant was a twenty-minute ride away, and she couldn't bear the thought of sitting through the entire ride without having something to sip on.

As she walked, she carefully tried to snap a picture of her cup against the city skyline, something for her, and her fans, to remember the day, her focus so attentive toward her phone that she failed to notice the man walking in her direction.

"Oops, sorry!" he said when he bumped into her.

"Hey, watch it! You almost made me spill my drink. This is a five-hundred-dollar dress, you know?" she loudly exclaimed, barely looking up.

"Oh, trust me, I do know."

"What?"

But when Tara looked up, she didn't see the scruffy drug addict she had expected to see. She didn't see a homeless man with ripped clothing and torn shoes. Instead, she saw a god, with his dark hair, deep eyes, and toned chest. She could barely keep her eyes off him.

"Hi," she said. "I'm Tara."

"Declan." He reached a hand out to shake hers. "Sorry again for knocking into you. I guess they don't call me 'clumsy two shoes' for nothing." He laughed, his smile so affectionate that it made her smile.

Tara shook her head. "No, it's my fault. I should've paid attention to where I was going." She placed her phone back into her purse and tucked it close to her.

"So, where you headed? What do you say I make it up to you by buying you dinner?"

He was definitely as charming as he was handsome, and if Tara wasn't married, she would've definitely jumped at the chance.

"Sorry, I can't. I'm actually meeting my husband for dinner. And I should really get going. I'm running late as it is."

His face fell; a look of disappointment washed over. "Aw, shucks, I should've known a pretty girl like you was taken. Well, shit out of luck, I guess. At least, let me give you my number. If you ever change your mind, you'll know who to call."

He smoothly pulled a pen out from his pocket and wrote his number on her coffee cup. "Such a shame, such a shame."

"Sorry," she said with a meek smile. "It was nice meeting you. I gotta run."

"Nice meeting you too, Tara Bardot. I'll see you around."

Tara scrunched her face when she walked away. She couldn't remember telling him her last name, and it was odd that he knew. But maybe she had. Maybe she introduced herself as such and had just forgotten. That could've very well been possible. Either way, she didn't have time to focus on it now. She needed to get there before Rowan murdered her.

Nearly thirty minutes later, she finally arrived. It didn't take long for her to spot her husband after walking in. He was sitting in their usual spot, with at least six empty glasses in front of him.

"Hey, babe, I'm sorry I'm—"

"Save it, Tara," he interrupted her, holding up a hand. "It's always the same excuse with you. You were supposed to be here two hours ago. Where the hell were you?"

"It's not my fault. I swear! The subway was running late, and it was so packed that I had to wait for the next train. I tried to get here as fast as I could. I promise!"

Rowan raised a brow as he took a sip of his drink. "Oh, is that so?"

"Yes!"

"Because it's way past rush hour. You shouldn't have been fighting with anyone."

"Well… I guess it's just a busy day today. It *is* Thursday night, after all. Everyone's probably getting a head start on their weekend."

"Uh huh, sure. Anything else you wanna lie to me about?"

"Babe, Rowan, what do you mean? I'm not lying to you! Let's just move past this and enjoy our anniversary." She reached her hands across the dinner table and grabbed onto his, holding them tight and running her finger across his wedding band. "So, what's my surprise this year? A diamond ring? A new purse? Ooo, did you get me that bracelet that all the celebrities are wearing? Imagine how popular I'd be if I wore that on stream."

But instead of gripping her hands back, he pulled his away. "No, Tara, you're not getting any of that. And frankly, I'm sick and tired of you spending all your time on social media. It feels like your relationship is more with your followers than with me. I don't even feel like your husband half the time, always being pushed aside when you need to stream or record. Can't you just put down the camera for once and live? Not everything in your life needs to be recorded, especially not our home."

"You know I can't do that. It's my lifestyle. It's how I make money. Of all people, you should understand that."

"Yeah, but can't you take a day off once in a while? Do you really need to be on *every day?*" He was now cutting into his steak, scarfing it down like he'd been waiting all day to eat. "Even now, you keep glancing over at your phone. Just put it away for the rest of the night. We're having dinner."

"I… I can't. Please don't hate me, but I'm actually supposed to live stream our anniversary dinner. Everyone's expecting it."

Rowan's eyes when she said that turned into flames. The calm expression on his face turned almost demonic, and he gritted his teeth so vigorously that she was afraid his teeth would pop out from their sockets. He pulled the cloth napkin off from his lap, wiped his mouth, and tossed it against his plate.

"I'm done, Tara. We're done. It's over."

She quickly turned off her camera and shot a look up at him. "What? What are you talking about? Are we leaving already?"

"No, I am. I've been having doubts about us for a while now, and this dinner was supposed to remedy that. But all you seem to care about are people you don't even know. I'm divorcing you, Tara. And truth is, I've actually started seeing someone else."

"What?!" Her scream was so loud and disruptive that half the restaurant turned to look at them. "You're cheating on me? What the fuck, Rowan?! Six years, and you're just going to throw it all down the drain?!"

"Oh, Tara, don't act so surprised. You knew it was happening, so much that you've turned your attention to other men. We're not good for each other. Never have been. I'm just sad it took me this long to figure it out."

As he walked away, Tara grabbed onto her husband's arm. "Stop! I'm not seeing other men. I'm not even interested in them."

"Really?" He nodded his head toward her cup, Declan's number written in large letters across it. "Say hi to Declan for me, and let him know how full of shit you are."

"HEY, WAKE UP, SLEEPY HEAD!" A pillow landed on Tara's face the next morning. She groaned and pushed it aside, her head pounding from the bottle she drank directly from last night.

After Rowan left her, he forced her to move out. She tried to fight it, but eventually had to accept that since she didn't have a hand in paying for any part of the house, she didn't deserve to keep it. Nor did she get to keep all the gifts he had gotten for her. Not the designer shoes. Not the luxury handbags. Not even the Gucci dresses taking up residency in her closet.

Though, she did manage to convince him to let her keep her camera setup. She needed her equipment more than she needed anything in her life. More than she needed him. And she wondered why he threw her out.

Luckily, her roommate from college was able to take her in, temporarily anyway. She was getting ready to move to San Francisco soon, but offered to help Tara find a place before she left. Ashley Simms had always been a party girl, taking Tara out right after the breakup and ordering her an entire bottle service before taking her back to her place and letting her crash on the couch. And though it was usually more than Tara could handle, it sure beat crying over a man and sleeping on the street.

"Are you ever going to stop throwing pillows at me? We're not in college anymore."

Ashley paused for a second. "Hmm, nope!" And she threw another one, this one much rougher than the last.

"Ouch! Dude, that hurts!"

"Oh, stop being such a baby. Come on, get up. It's way past noon. Let's go get some food. Sleeping all day isn't going to make all your problems go away."

"No!" Tara grabbed her blanket and pulled it over her head. "I'm not sleeping. I'm mentally preparing for my stream later tonight. I need to get ready to tell my followers about my divorce." She yanked the blanket up further. "Ugh!! It's too stressful."

Ashley sat down beside her and tried to tug the sheet off, but with no luck. "Hey! I have an idea.

Why don't you *not* stream for one night, especially not about something as personal as a divorce? I always thought Rowan was an arrogant jerk, and as much as I hated him, he does have a point. You spend *way* too much time broadcasting your personal life. Maybe keep a few things private."

That's when the sheet shot off. "Time off? Time *off?!* You're just like him. You don't understand. None of you do. This is my *lifestyle!* I'm an influencer, remember? I *have* to stream and go live every day, share my life even if I don't want to. It's my livelihood. If I don't, I lose it all. You just don't know what it's like having the world follow you. It's a lot of pressure."

Ashley rolled her eyes. "Whatever, Tara. Not my thing, and will never be my thing. It's just not real enough for me." Then she jumped on top of her friend. "But you know what is real? That stack of pancakes waiting for me at Denny's. Come on, let's go!"

One Night Stand

Chapter Two
DECLAN

"HELLO?" DECLAN HAYES ANSWERED his phone while crossing the busy streets of Times Square.

Thursday evenings were usually his most hectic times. He worked the night shift as a tech specialist at one of the largest social media corporations in the country, overseeing all the daily interactions and ensuring that the platform doesn't come crashing down again like it did just three months ago.

He was already late as is. Being the most eligible bachelor in all of New York City was no easy task. The women he saw always wanted to go to the same places at the same time, and he struggled just keeping up with two, let alone five. And of course, they never wanted to leave when he needed them to.

He had a job to get to, but his dates would much rather hoard him for themselves and spend the evenings drinking. As much as he'd like to do the latter, he could never be around these chicks for too long. Their neediness drove him insane, and sometimes, he was glad he had a job to use for his excuse.

"Mr. Matthews, sorry, I'm running a little late. I'll be there in five minutes. Max!" He said on his phone to his boss, adding a little bounce and speed to his steps.

"Don't even bother, Hayes," the voice on the other line shouted back. "I'm getting really tired of your excuses. Don't even bother. You're fired."

As the sound of human voice turned to a screeching buzz, Declan almost wanted to walk into the office anyway and clock in, not at his computer, but at his boss' face. Why'd he need a job anyway?

Companies were always full of nothing but pricks who are stuck in the nose and play games with their employees, treating them as valuable members of the team one minute and letting them go the next. Sure, he'd come in late every now and then, take three-hour lunch breaks, and spend most of his time on his phone, but that didn't mean he deserved to be treated like garbage.

It was nearly 8pm; the night was still early, and he didn't know how to utilize his free time. His usual routine was to go to work and then head over to the lounge by 2am. He was a regular at Dirty Dancing, and it'd be weird for him to show up so early. He didn't even think it opened until close to midnight. As he walked over to the nearest cart to buy himself a hot dog, he spotted a familiar face.

Wait, is that Tara Bardot? He turned to the vendor. "Hey, dude, is that Tara Bardot?"

But the vendor, a pimply-faced teenage boy, just stared at him and shrugged. "How the hell should I know? Now, hand over the cash. I don't do freebies."

Declan sighed, digging a hand into his pocket, and pulled out his wallet. "How much?"

The boy whacked the sign on the side of the cart with his tongs. "Can't you read? Two bucks."

"Here." He nodded his head toward the condiments. "Some mustard, too. And don't skimp out."

"Dude, you gotta pay extra for that."

Declan raised a brow. "Are you serious, kid?"

"A dollar. Or no mustard."

"Aw, come on, kid. I just got laid off. Give a guy a break, will ya?"

"A dollar. Or no mustard," he repeated.

"Fuck, dude. Fine, just give me the dog."

When Declan walked away, shaking his head, he bit into his hot dog. It was dry and tasteless, the texture so foreign and off-putting in his mouth as he wrestled to swallow the remainder of the bun. When he finished, thirty seconds later, he was left feeling even hungrier than he had been before.

"Hey, Tara, over here! Over here!" He heard close by.

Declan turned his head to where the voice was coming from and saw Tara taking a picture with a little girl.

Tara, he thought. *I knew that was her.*

He waited for a few minutes before walking over to her. He couldn't seem too suspicious by cornering her in a coffee shop. So, he waited. And waited. And waited. Plotting his next move for when she came out. He had to make it seem like a coincidence.

"Oops, sorry!" he said, bumping into her.

"Hey, watch it! You almost made me spill my drink. This is a five-hundred-dollar dress, you know?" she exclaimed.

Even though she didn't make eye contact, she still looked as stunning as ever, her diamond earrings shining bright, and her revealing dress enough to make him drool.

"Oh, trust me, I do know."

"What?"

Word fart. He didn't want Tara knowing that he knew who she was. He wanted their meeting to be fated, like the stars drove them together on this fateful night. He couldn't let her know that he'd been watching her.

"Hi," she said. "I'm Tara."

"Declan." He reached a hand out to shake hers. The skin of her hand was smooth and soft, like a baby's bottom. "Sorry again for knocking into you. I guess they don't call me 'clumsy two shoes' for nothing." He laughed, rubbing the back of his neck in hopes of concealing his awkwardness.

Tara shook her head. "No, it's my fault. I should've paid attention to where I was going."

She placed her phone back into her purse and held the bag close to her body. He could tell that she was obviously nervous about their conversation. He *was* coming off a little strong, but maybe she wouldn't mind him taking one step closer.

"So, where you headed? What do you say I make it up to you by buying you dinner?" He smiled as he spoke, his white teeth grinning through his charming smile, hoping it was enough to entice her.

"Sorry, I can't. I'm actually meeting my husband for dinner. And I should really get going. I'm running late as it is."

His face fell; a look of disappointment washed over. "Aw, shucks, I should've known a pretty girl like you was taken. Well, shit out of luck, I guess. At least, let me give you my number. If you ever change your mind, you'll know who to call."

He felt around his back pocket and pulled out a ballpoint pen. He then grabbed her coffee cup and wrote his number on it. "Such a shame, such a shame."

"Sorry," she said with a smile. "It was nice meeting you. I gotta run."

"Nice meeting you too, Tara Bardot. I'll see you around."

He felt a pin prick to his heart as she skipped away. *Husband? I mean, I'm not surprised, but damn, did she really have to throw it in my face like that?*

His thoughts were interrupted when his phone rang again. He fumbled it out from his pocket, hoping that his son-of-a-bitch boss had decided to change his mind and let him have his job back. Instead, he saw a number he didn't recognize on his phone. It could be anyone. A telemarketer. A hacker. His mom. He sure as hell didn't know. He was never one to keep numbers. Memorizing them were a waste of time, and plus, if he did, he wouldn't have an excuse to turn women away after a hookup. A simple no strings attached one-night stand.

He sighed. They all wanted the same thing with him. A relationship. But that was something he wanted to stay as far away from as possible. He didn't believe in relationships. Love, sure. He could fall in love with someone but still not be in a relationship with them. That was definitely possible. But once a woman wants to spend more time with him and claim him as her own, that's where he drew the line. He could never picture himself being tied down like that, not again. Not after the last time.

Serena Taylor was the love of his life. They met in Venice seven years ago, when he was taking a gap year in between jobs, and she was studying abroad. He was a man of impulsiveness and possibilities, and she was a naïve student ready to venture out into the world of responsibility. It was Declan's last day there, the end to a miserable trip of loneliness, self-regret, and terrible weather. He thought a quick escape would help him forget about losing one of the only jobs he'd ever loved. But it's true what they say. He never really could escape from his problems, his woes hopping on a plane with him and sleeping beside him in his hotel room.

On his last day, he vowed to never visit Italy, or any country for that matter, ever again once he hopped back onto the plane and back to the states. Traveling felt like such a waste of time to him, a money-sucking waste of time with absolutely no reward. But that all changed when he met her, a gorgeous blonde bombshell who took one look at him and struggled to look away. And it was in that moment that he fell in love with Italy again.

Their affair was passionate. They both wanted each other like they were two ravenous wolves reaching for the same piece of filet mignon, and after just one passionate night, they became inseparable, holding hands whenever they went and tearing off each other's clothes whenever they had the chance. Declan never expected a relationship to come out of a one-night stand, but it did, and he didn't complain. Not one bit.

Neither of them expected a blossoming romance when they each stepped foot into the country, and neither of them expected their passionate fling to spiral into more than that. She moved into his apartment in the heart of Manhattan, and together, they traveled the world. Her love for culture and global scenery enticed him, and he fell so blindly in love that he was willing to follow her anywhere. Thailand. Switzerland. Ireland. And so much more, branding each country before they said their farewells. Serena Taylor. Declan was so sure that she was the woman he wanted to marry and spend the rest of his life with.

But soon, things turned dark. Serene began disappearing at odd hours of the night, saying she had to visit her sick parents or her heartbroken friend.

"I'm spending the night there," she would say. "Don't wait up."

And still naïve and clueless, Declan believed her. For six whole months, he believed her. Her lies. It wasn't until he found out about Nicolas Blake did his life begin to fall apart.

"Who the fuck were you kissing? Answer me, Serena! Who the fuck were you making out with?"

She crossed her arms over her chest in denial. "What are you even talking about? I wasn't kissing anyone!"

"Don't lie to me, Serena. I followed you. I saw you. Who is he?"

He knew he wouldn't like the answer she'd give. Whatever came out of her mouth, he'd hate it either way.

"You're following me? Where the hell do you get off following me?! That's an invasion of my rights!"

He should've stopped there, stopped prodding, but she was his first true love, and he couldn't let it go. He couldn't let her go.

"You don't have rights when you're in a relationship, especially not when it involves your partner. Tell me!"

"My husband, okay?! He's my husband."

Suddenly, it all made sense, why she wanted to spend time with him when they were no longer in the country, why she always disappeared in the middle of the night. *He* was the other person, the homewrecker.

Declan never spoke to Serena again after she moved out. She packed up all her belongings and moved to the cozy city of Phoenix, Arizona. As for her husband, she left him, the guilt of never being able to stay loyal to him wreaking havoc on her mind, swearing to never hurt another man like she did to him and Declan. But a month after she settled into her new home, there was already another man in her arms.

"That lying bitch," Declan muttered to himself when his mind returned to the present.

The sound of his ringtone was enough to make anyone turn their head; vulgar slurs and offensive taunts were never someone's first choice, but for Declan, they were something he could never live without.

"I thought I blocked her," he whispered quietly when he saw Angela's name appear on his screen.

He quickly rejected the call and proceeded to swipe up, rhythmically moving through his screens until he found the button he needed... as if he'd done it many times before.

Angela was his most recent hookup, among others. Most of them usually got the hint that he wasn't interested when he threw their shoes out in the middle of the dead night. But Angela, no, she wasn't like the others; she was completely clueless. Instead, seeing her shoes on his wet front lawn gave her the message that she needed to go retrieve them, dry them off with Declan's only clean towel, and climb back into bed with him.

He scoffed. "Clueless. Fucking clueless."

As he went to put his phone away, another message popped up. This time, from his dating app.

Kaitlyn Starr: Hey, Declan. Checked out your profile. Looking slick. What do ya say we get together some time?

A smile glazed over his face. Kaitlyn was hot, not a perfect ten, but she'd do.

Declan Hayes: Grab a drink? Twenty minutes, club on 22nd. Be there.

He closed his message with a wink before sending it off, shoving his phone back into his pocket and heading over. He didn't even bother to check whether she was on board. He never did. If she showed, great. If not, then he was sure he could find another warm body to spend the night with.

Chapter Three
TARA

ASHLEY POKED HER FRIEND ON the arm as she nudged her. "Tara, girl, you gotta stop obsessing. Stalking your ex isn't going to help you move on."

"But… but… why's he so damn happy anyway? What the hell does she have that I don't?" "Um… let's see… a life?" Ashley grabbed her sweater off the back of her chair and chucked it across the room, landing it on her couch cushion.

"I just don't understand." Tara took a sip of her coffee and let out a long sigh. "He told me he was fine with my lifestyle when I first started. He thought it was a great career, working for myself. What changed? Why'd he choose this slut over me?"

She pointed to a picture of Rowan's new girlfriend, wearing a summer dress and flashing a pearly white smile that could blind anyone who wasn't careful.

Rowan didn't care much for social media… which was why Tara struggled for weeks trying to find out what he was up to. It wasn't until one of her fans, no less obsessive than her, sent her a link to Faith Auburn's page did she discover that he'd been shacking it up with some woman in Boston ever since she moved out.

"He didn't even have the balls to tell me he was leaving New York. How dare he?!" she had said when she found out, though, no one seemed to side with her, only a few of her followers.

"Could be because she's not as obsessed with her image and social media," Ashley responded. She glared over Tara's shoulder, looking at the same picture she was. "I mean, look at her. She barely posts once a week, and she has no problem walking out without a face covered in makeup. She's just an average girl. Didn't you tell me it's what Rowan always wanted?"

Tara gave her a deadly glare. "Whose side are you on anyway?"

"Whoa, whoa, don't come after me! I didn't break your heart." Ashley threw her arms in the air and stepped back. "All I'm saying is, maybe if you step away from social media once in a while, you won't run into this problem again. Believe it or not, not everyone is as obsessed with the Internet as you are."

"Ashley! Stop! You're supposed to be supporting me! Not judging me! You're supposed to be my friend!"

"Alright, fine, fine. I'm sorry. But it's really hard supporting someone who spends fifteen hours a day stalking their ex. Why don't you start with putting the phone down?"

She reached over and tried to grab Tara's phone from her hands, but she had to learn the hard way that that just wasn't going to happen.

"Back off!" Tara hissed at her friend and pushed back her chair. She stood up, fingers still swiping through Faith's photos, and sat herself down on the couch, eyes never leaving the screen. "Besides, I haven't streamed in weeks. I've lost thousands of followers who expect me to be there for them, and here I am chasing after some man I don't even like anymore, and my life is nothing but a big, FAT MESS!"

She threw her phone down, grabbed a throw pillow, and smothered her face under it. "I had everything! A rich husband. Fans, fucking fans! And the life I've always wanted. And now, look at me! I'm a loser, a dried-up hack sleeping on my best friend's couch, and I'll forever be alone. Forever!"

Ashley stood up from her chair and walked over to the couch to console her friend. She placed her mug on the coffee table in front of her and rested a hand on Tara's leg.

"No, honey, you're not a loser. You're just going through a rough patch right now. You've been so consumed by the Internet that you feel lost without it, and lost without a man dangling off your arm. But trust me, it'll get better. I promise."

Tara shifted the pillow from her face. "You sure?"

Ashley nodded. "But first, you need to take a serious shower and change your clothes."

Getting up on her feet, Tara walked over to the small mirror hanging by the front door. Her friend was right. The stained sweatpants, smeared makeup, and tangled hair weren't doing anyone any favors. She brushed a strand of her blonde hair away from her mouth, tugging at it gently to release it from the crusted lipstick still decorating her lips.

"Yeah, maybe you're right. Maybe I did let myself go."

"Of course, I'm right! And after you clean yourself up, we're getting you in some guy's bed. Forget about Rowan. Fuck the memories away, and when you wake up again, you'll be back to your old self."

Tara gave her a skeptical look, one eyebrow raised much higher than the other. "I don't know… Ash. I've done those dating sites before I married Rowan, and nothing but trouble ever came out of th—"

"No, no, no! It's different!" Ashley ran over to the kitchen counter and grabbed her phone. "It's new. A coworker was talking about it during lunch the other day. It's purely for hookups. No strings attached. You literally meet up, bang it out, and you'll never have to see each other again… unless you want to, of course."

"I don't know… what if someone doesn't play by the rules? I'm really not in the mood for another crazy ex."

"Trust me, Tara, nothing bad will happen. It's all for fun. Everyone on the app knows it. It's a win-win!" She winked. "Besides, I may have tested out the waters a couple times."

"You?!" Tara exclaimed. "I thought you had such a huge crush on Mark that no one could ever replace him!"

A blush washed over Ashley's face as she turned her eyes slightly away. "And no one ever can. Doesn't mean I have to be celibate while waiting around for him to notice me. Ah, Mark..." She propped her chin onto the palm of her hand, and her elbow onto one arm of the couch. "How can I ever replace those sexy brown eyes and that chiseled chin?" Her face blanked, and her voice fell silent as her thoughts drifted elsewhere.

"Snap out of it!"

"Huh? Oh, right. Anyway, what I was saying is, just go out for one night and have a little fun. Just one. And if you hate it, I'll never pressure you again. But after six years of being married to the same dude, you gotta go out and just let loose. Fuck the first guy you meet. Let it all out, and," she grabbed the phone away from Tara's hands, "it's time you stop stalking Rowan. He's with someone else. You need to let it go, and stop this obsession."

"Fine, you're right. I'll give it a shot. But *I* get to choose the guy, and *you* don't get to meddle. Got it?"

"Not a word from me." Ashley pretended to zip her mouth shut.

"So, what's this dumb app called anyway?" Tara began to rapidly swipe through her apps to get to the store. "Dating…"

The room fell silent. Ashley was nowhere to be heard as Tara continued to explore the hundreds of different dating apps. "Ash?"

Not a sound was heard.

"Ash!" Tara whipped her head up and saw her friend, still with a pretend zipper over her mouth. She rolled her eyes, "You can talk."

"Whew!" Ashley let out a sigh. "Good riddance!" She scooted herself closer to where Tara was sitting on the couch. "Alright, let's see… it starts with an X…"

Within minutes, a profile was created, and Tara found herself scrolling through pages upon pages of eligible bachelors.

"Ooo, that guy's cute!" Ashley pointed to a blonde guy with a sparkling smile who likes to spend his time running and hiking.

"I thought you weren't gonna meddle! Besides, he's too active for me. I like to maintain a sedentary lifestyle."

"You know you're just gonna fuck him, right? No one's forcing you to go on a five-mile run."

"I know," Tara said as she continued to scroll. "But I like to keep my options open in case we happen to get along."

"You mean, in case he has a good dick?" Ashley teased.

"Shut up! Jackpot! Found someone. 6'2, muscular, sexy-ass eyes, and during his free time, he's… a social media influencer?! No way!"

Now, it was time for Ashley to roll her eyes. "Of course, you pick out the one guy who's EXACTLY like you. What's his name?"

"Declan Hayes." She paused. "Why does that name sound so familiar?"

"Probably one of your millions and millions of fans. I swear, I don't know how you keep up with them. I would literally blow my brains out if I woke up to thousands of emails in one day."

"You're probably right. I'm just being paranoid."

Tara Bardot: Hey, Declan! I'm Tara. Wanna grab a drink later?

Chapter Four
TARA

"ARE YOU SURE WE'RE IN the right bar?!" Ashley shouted over the blaring music as she walked into Club Moonstone with Tara lingering behind her.

"I think so?" Tara shouted back. "I tripled check the message, and he told me to meet him here!"

"Even if he is here, it's way too crowded to find anyone. Tell you what, you got my number. Call me if you need anything. I'll be chowing down some pizzas next door." She turned around to leave before turning back. "And remember, shoot me a text before you run off with the guy back to his place. I'd rather not spend more time than I need to in this part of town."

"Yeah, yeah, I know. Girls' code, remember?" Tara waved her off, and Ashley walked away.

As Tara watched her friend squeeze through a crowd of frat boys and horny housewives, she looked around the club, suddenly feeling extremely alone and out of place. She made her way toward the restroom, bobbing and weaving her body through the crowd like Ashley did earlier, trying her best to avoid entering a threesome or wearing vomit as her new couture.

The wooden door was off its hinge and nearly torn to shreds when she eventually found it, stepping over a girl squirming on the floor about her dad who abandoned her as a child, and squeezing in between two plump chicks trying to put on matching lipsticks, to get to a mirror. She turned on the sink, the cold chill of the water not nearly as bothersome as it had been in the past, and splashed a sprinkle of water over both sides of her face.

"Get it together, Tara. You came here for a reason. No backing out now!" she told her reflection.

"First time here?" A voice beside her suddenly spoke up.

Tara spun her head around and saw a woman smoking a cigarette standing beside her. She had a short black pixie cut with hot pink highlights messily placed, and her nose ring was so loud and large that Tara could barely look at her without chuckling.

"What do you mean?" she asked instead, holding back her laughter.

"Name's Debbie, but you can call me Deb. We all know why you're here. It's why the rest of us are all here." She nodded. "You just don't seem like the type who'd come to a place like this?" She leaned in closer. "Between you and me, this is more of a place for horny middle-aged woman and ugly chicks. I just come here to get high once in a while." She stepped back. "Who's the lucky guy?"

"Declan Hayes."

The girl's mouth fell open, the cigarette spiraling out of her mouth. "Declan Hayes? THE Declan Hayes?"

Tara gave her a perplexed look, as if she'd just walked into a world where names could kill. "Yeah…?"

"You need to leave! Get out of here fast before he notices you. Declan's a very, very dangerous man."

"What? Dangerous? I don't understand. Do you know him?"

"He's my—"

Suddenly, the restroom door flew open, and at least ten women came rushing in, all heading toward the stalls.

"What? He's your what?" Tara shouted over to Debbie, hoping to catch her answer, but with both the sound and the crowd, Debbie was gone. Completely out of sight.

Anxiety began to build in Tara's mind, that maybe Debbie was telling her the truth, and she should really stay clear of him. She thought about heading out the back door, walking away and joining Ashley next door, but part of her refused to let him go.

"She's probably just his ex or something. A jealous ex who doesn't want anyone else near him. I'm sure it's nothing to worry about."

She didn't know what to do. Walking back and forth between the dance floor and the back door, pacing as she ruminated over her thoughts. Suddenly, a hand tapped her shoulder.

DECLAN

DECLAN ROLLED OVER ON HIS BED, hoping to grab his pillow and snuggle back to sleep with it. He was surprised when he grabbed a female breast instead, the feeling of squishy human skin enough to make him perk open his eyes and jump out of bed.

"Jesus, Kaitlyn! What the fuck are you still doing here?" His face fumed red, then turned pale when he realized that nothing was covering the lower half of his body, and he quickly dropped his pillow over it.

Kaitlyn giggled. "Silly, pickle. I know what your dick looks like." She reached across the bed and tugged on the pillow. "And I especially know what it feels like… inside me." She winked.

"Kaitlyn, stop! I mean it!" He yelled as he fought the pillow away from her. Declan was much, much stronger, and one tug too hard sent Kaitlyn tumbling onto the ground. "And I'm not your pickle."

"What the hell?" Kaitlyn stumbled as she tried to stand the first time, tripping over the sheet of the bed and falling back down. When she finally managed to get back onto her feet, she gave Declan a light smack on his thick arm and said, "Stop messing around, pickle. I know you'll never hurt me. Now, how about you come back to bed, and I'll give you a *special* massage." She winked at him and grabbed his hand.

But instead, he yanked it away. "I said, stop calling me that! And I want you out of my house before I call the cops."

"Geez, what's biting your ass? Just last night, you said you could see yourself spending the rest of your life with me. What happened to that?"

"Gone. Dead. All of it. Please leave."

Slowly and heartbroken, Kaitlyn swung her bare legs over the bed and dragged herself off. She bent down to retrieve her bra, and as she did, Declan couldn't help but grow stiff staring at the way her tight naked body glowed in the sunlight. But he knew he had to be strong. He didn't have feelings for this girl; it's all physical. And he knew that one slip of the tongue could cause her to climb back into bed. No, he couldn't have that.

"What's with all these pictures of Tara Bardot?" Kaitlyn asked as she found herself staring at Declan's office area. She chuckled, "I thought only little girls liked her. You suddenly into makeup and fashion?"

Declan's eyes widened. He quickly rushed over to Kaitlyn and pushed her toward the front door, one final nudge to get her to the other side. "Bye, Kaitlyn." Without waiting for an answer, he slammed the door in her face.

He turned back around, coming face-to-face with the pictures on his wall. No one else was supposed to see this. This was supposed to be his own secret, his dark secret hidden from the rest of the world. From the base of his desk up to the ceiling, and encompassing an entire wall, were pictures of Tara Bardot, with images taken directly from her social media page to screenshots of her streams; Declan had an entire memorial dedicated to the influencer herself. He reached out and tugged off a picture of Tara in a bikini. *So smoking hot,* he thought. *If only you were mine.*

His phone rang, the sound of a message. He leapt onto his bed, still completely nude, and unlocked it. And there it was. Staring at him right in the face.

Tara Bardot: Hey, Declan! I'm Tara. Wanna grab a drink later?

TARA

"I THOUGHT YOU LOOKED familiar! Remember me?" The man behind her said when she spun around.

It took a minute for Tara to recognize the face staring back at her. "Declan? You wrote your number on my coffee cup."

"I did! And you never called me back!"

"I know. Sorry, things have been pretty rough the past few weeks."

He placed a hand on the small of her back. She shivered.

"Hey, no worries. Fate brought us together instead. I guess it's meant to be. What's your drink?" He gestured her toward the bar.

Tara tensed her shoulders as she followed him. She wasn't sure what to think. Sure, Declan was extremely handsome and such a gentleman, but she also partly blamed him for ruining her marriage.

If only he'd never written down his fucking number.

However, even if she didn't want to admit it, she knew that, deep down, her marriage was ruined way before she ever met Declan.

"Long Island," she said, giving him a weak smile.

"Talk to me, Tara."

"About what?"

"Last time I saw you, you were skirting away from me to meet your husband. Now, you're messaging me on a hookup app and chilling in the swankiest, and might I add, sexiest, club in all of New York City. What gives?"

"Things changed. I don't really wanna talk about it."

She took a sip of her drink. Her head started feeling woozy as she did, but she blamed the single granola bar she'd eaten the entire day, too nervous about her night out to really stomach anything else.

As her vision focused in and out, she could hardly make out the words he was saying, and it wasn't until he leaned over and kissed her did she remember where she was. He leaned into her ear, whispered a long slur followed by the word *place*, and led her off her seat and out the back door of the club.

"Wait… Ash…," Tara began to mumble, but before anyone could answer her, she found herself tripping on her heels as Declan led her into a cab parked outside.

The thirty-minute ride back to his place felt surreal, like her mind was floating outside her own body, soaring high in the sky and dancing in circles around the cab. It felt as if her ethereal self was trying to tell her something, but the blasting music and voracious slobbers of Declan's wet kisses on her neck and face distracted her, pulling her away from her own conscience.

"I'm gonna make you forget all about that husband of yours," he whispered into her ear as he nibbled on it.

She felt her body fall victim to his roaming hands, with all her inhibitions and wariness of who this man was completely thrown out the window and crushed under the public bus behind them. She let herself go, sinking to his every touch, and he knew it, dragging down the straps of her dress as his lips explored her shoulders.

When they finally arrived back to his apartment, Tara was already partially undressed. She giggled as she stepped out of the cab and tripped again. But luckily, Declan was there to catch her fall, his arms wrapped tightly around her waist.

"Whoa, there. You're a clumsy one, aren't ya?" He grinned at her as he spoke.

She could feel a sharp object pressing against her backside. A gun, perhaps? Or a knife? But when she quickly turned around and grabbed it, she found herself holding onto his crotch.

"Oh, sorry," she slurred. "Thought it was something else." And she quickly released her hand.

His grin grew even wider. "Someone's a little eager. Don't worry, darling. It's all yours."

He bent down and scooped her up in his arms, smacking a wet kiss on her lips, and brought her inside, refusing to put her down until they were both lying on his bed. She looked around, though her vision blurred. His room looked like any other room, with a simple mattress dressed with ugly gray sheets, an old computer, and completely bare walls; not even a painting was to be seen.

"Hey," he whispered, turning her head toward him.

He then leaned over and kissed her hard on the lips, inserting his tongue into hers and giving her the sloppiest kiss she ever had. She tried to pull away, but his grip grew tighter, and eventually, her doubts faded, her body submissive.

Tara jerked her body forward as Declan undid the zipper on the back of her dress. The feeling of his soft hands on the bare of her back was enough to make her tingle and shiver. He pulled her closer, his hands wrapping around the front and massaging her bare breasts as the dress naturally fell off, and she found herself wearing nothing but a thin laced thong, lying in front of a man she had just met.

She had always been shy around people, especially men she didn't know. It took her nearly six months before she finally drummed up the courage to take her clothes off in front of Rowan, and even then, she immediately jumped under the sheets once she realized what was happening.

But there was just something about Declan that felt… different, safe almost. It felt like she had known him his entire life, and as if he knew exactly how to take care of her and pleasure her in a way that she desired.

And when his body entered hers, their world instantly connected, not just physically, but she felt a sense that she belonged with him, that this man who was dick deep inside her was her soulmate, and that they were fated to meet. He felt so tender, so warm, so orgasmic, that all her worries and obsession with Rowan instantly melted from her mind, as she closed her eyes and let his body overtake hers.

One Night Stand

Chapter Five
TARA

THE NEXT MORNING, TARA found herself still in Declan's room, with the same ugly gray sheets and the same bare white walls. Her head was pounding, the feeling of a thousand migraines mixed together into one deadly concoction. She had dealt with hangovers before, the worst when she took eight tequila shots on an empty stomach at a frat party during her college days, but this? This was so much worse, as if a truck had smashed into her and shattered her body into a million pieces.

She rubbed her forehead with her hand, her fingers moist and sweaty as she made her way out of bed, the bedsheet wrapped around her, and into the bathroom.

"Declan?" she called out, washing her hands in the sink and splashing droplets of water over her face to wake herself up.

But the apartment remained silent, nothing but the sound of honking cabs outside.

"Ugh, I think I'm gonna be sick," she said quietly, turning her back to the door and hurling everything she had inside her straight into the toilet bowl. "Ugh," she said again, grabbing a towel off the rack and wiping her mouth.

She walked back into his room, trying to regain her composure and sober up before she walks out the door and probably collides with a truck. When she got to his doorway, she tripped on a wire and fell onto the floor, awaking his computer… with the monitor showing none other than Tara Bardot in a lime green bikini.

"What the fuck?" she whispered.

She tried to unlock his computer, to see what other dark secrets he was hiding, but twenty-six passwords later, she was still shit out of luck. And that's when she noticed a photo sticking out of the left drawer of his desk, a photo with a familiar print, similar to her designer wedding dress.

She pulled open the drawer and fished it out. It was a picture of her and Rowan on their wedding day, only, his face had been cut out and replaced by Declan's. Vomit stewed in her stomach and rose up into her mouth, the acid burning her throat as it traveled. She couldn't believe what she was seeing. This man, this deliciously gorgeous man she had only just met for a night of fun, was… was obsessed with her.

Terrified, her hands shaking, she rummaged through the rest of the drawer, finding piles upon piles of photos of herself, from her social media posts to her streams to her everyday life. Hell, she even found a picture of herself sitting on a plane with Rowan, wearing the fluorescent pink tracksuit she wore when they took that trip to Maui.

"Oh, god…," she whispered, dropping the photos from her hand.

He wasn't only obsessed with her; he was stalking her.

"Looking for something?" A voice startled her, and she jumped. It was the devil himself.

"Uh… no, not at all," she stuttered. "Listen, last night was super, but I really have to get going."

She slammed the pictures back into the drawer and grabbed her clothes off the floor, not even bothering to dress herself as she made her way through the doorway.

She should've known he wasn't going to let her go that easily.

"What's the rush, darling? Just last night, you were screaming my name so loud I thought my neighbors were going to call the cops, and now, you're trying to leave?" He pouted. "And here I was thinking you liked me."

"I-I-I do," she stuttered, digging for words she could say to get her out of this alive. "I-I do like you, a lot, actually. I just have to get to a very important meeting right now." She flashed him a smile. "How about we meet up later? Dinner?"

He thought about it, his fingers playing with the facial hair on his chin. "Or…," he began. "You could skip your meeting, and we can spend all day in bed. Tell you what, I'll even cook us spaghetti with fresh crab meat for dinner tonight. I know it's your favorite."

"H-H-How did you know that? I never told you what my favorite dish is."

He shrugged, unfazed by her surprise. "Just a lucky guess. Doesn't take much for soulmates to figure each other out."

Tara felt drops of sweat drip down her back. She knew she had to get the hell out of this place, but Declan wasn't going to just allow it without a fight. She needed a plan, an excuse, something to let someone know that she was in trouble.

Ashley.

She threw a fake smile over at him, dropping the sheet she still had wrapped around her naked body, and grazed her fingers against his shoulder.

"You're right, Declan, sweetie, totally right. I'd love to stay here with you, spend all day in bed eating ice cream and watching movies. Sounds like a dream." She leaned up and gave him a peck on the cheek. "How about you take your clothes off, I'll cancel my meeting, and then I'll join you in bed? Just the two of us."

"Now that's what I'm talking about."

As Declan quickly stripped the garments off his body, his groin enlarged, and the muscles of his upper thighs protruded. Tara forced her eyes away in search for her phone.

"C'mon, where is it?"

She looked inside her purse, but found it completely empty. She didn't even care about her keys and wallet at this point; she was just so desperate to get out. She looked under the bed, shoving aside the pizza boxes and empty soda cans, but came up short also.

"Hey, Declan," she said. "Have you seen my phone?"

"Yeah," he replied, biting into a protein bar he magically pulled out of the air. "Saw it. Burned it."

"You did WHAT?!"

She couldn't believe what he had just said. Not only was he clearly clinically insane, but he was also a psychopath. She fumed, her face turning red. How could someone so charming and handsome turn out to be such a monster?

"Burned it," he repeated. "Didn't think you'd need it. Besides, you said you're staying here. Who cares if you're a no-show?"

"I care! You had no right to do that!"

Rage overcame her, and she grabbed the nearest vodka bottle she could find and hurled it at him. It missed, but the glass shattered against the wall around him, temporarily disabling him. Tara quickly threw her clothes on, tucked her shoes underneath her arm, and headed out the door. The one-story apartment wasn't that big, and the front door was in plain sight. All she needed to do was make it a few more steps, and she'd be free.

But the lock was jammed. Of course, of all the times this could've happened, the lock was jammed. She jiggled it, twisting and turning it in all possible ways to try and free herself. She was usually so skilled at figuring these things out, but her sweaty fingers were definitely her enemy right now. After a few more tries, she heard a click, and then her world turned dark.

TARA WOKE UP SEVERAL HOURS LATER, her wrists chained to the frame of Declan's bed. She tried to tug one loose, but the sharp metal cut against her skin instead, sending a trail of blood dripping down her arm. She looked down at her body, naked once again, with only a single pink collar wrapped around her neck.

"Declan!" she screamed at the top of her lungs. She knew she should never have trusted Ashley. That dumb app turned out to be nothing but her own personal nightmare. "One night of fun, my ass," she grumbled.

Her stomach soon growled, and she realized she hadn't eaten since early yesterday. The little she had stored as nourishment in her stomach turned into nothingness when she hurled everything left inside her straight into the monster's toilet bowl. Her head was still wobbly from when he'd whacked her across the skull with what felt like an extremely heavy textbook, and she could feel the crusted blood on where it had dried up.

While she was knocked out, she reminisced back to when she lived a stable life with a stable partner in a stable relationship. It was six months after she said her vows to Rowan, and life couldn't be better for the both of them. He was gentle yet strong, understanding yet spoke up about his own opinions, and she saw in him herself. They loved each other, spending night and day together, promising each other they'd be in each other's lives forever.

But then it all changed. She changed, at least. Her world was turned toward the side of a necessary evil when she discovered Winks, the hot new social media platform that came charging into town on an angry bull. She'd never cared much about the Internet or an online presence before, but when her cousin introduced her to it, she became instantly hooked, building a large following and refusing to quit even as she saw her marriage quickly drift apart.

"Who's hungry??" Declan interrupted her memories as he came charging into the room, a platter of tea and biscuits in one hand and a couple napkins in the other. The pure irony.

He knelt down and handed her a biscuit, but she turned her head away. He then tried to feed her, but she bit down on his hand instead.

"Ouch!" he yelped as he winced and pulled back.

He ran out of the room to run his hand under cold water, soothing the wound. When he returned, he stared deeply at the sight of his own blood dripping down her chin, and she spat out the remains onto his rug.

"Feisty, are we?"

Instead of the anger she had expected from him, from any normal person in this situation, he smirked. He leaned down next to her and stroked her hair, planting kisses along her shoulders and neck.

"Get away from me, you fucking PIG!" she yelled, jerking her body away, but he was too strong.

He pinned her against the bed and tugged hard on her hair. "Don't you dare fucking talk to me like that!"

His face was growing hot, and his eyeballs looked ready to pop out from their sockets. But then it turned. As quickly as his expression turned from passion to anger, it now turned… turned… almost maniac.

He cackled as he stood up, slapping her across the face and walking away. He moved over to his desk, opened a drawer, and pulled out a picture.

"Ah, I remember this day." His expression now turned soft and mellow. He ran his fingers over what looked like two people in the photo. "I had just gotten my job offer, one of the happiest days of my life, when I saw you, wearing the sexiest red sequin dress I had every laid eyes on. Your curves were in all the right places, your breasts plump. It was just too bad that you were still with… him.

"What?"

But then Tara remembered. The night of her two-year anniversary with Rowan. Winks had been on the market for a little over a year, and Tara's following skyrocketed to unreachable numbers. Rowan decided to take her out to the fanciest restaurant to celebrate, a night of champagne and lobsters.

Had he seen me?

"You… you were there?" she asked, her voice trembling.

Declan gave her a smile that sent chills up and down her spine. "Oh, darling. Of course, I was. I'm *always* there."

"But… but… I don't understand. Why are you doing this? Why are you following me? What do you WANT FROM ME?!"

His expression now dropped, like a sad puppy who just found out he isn't getting fed. "Aw, no, darling. I don't want anything from you." He leaned down and gave her a hug.

She felt herself submitting to his arms; the warmth of his body sent a certain sense of comfort through her.

Maybe he wasn't so bad after all. Maybe he was just lonely and needed someone to love.

She loosened her shoulders and pulled closer to him, allowing him to lean down and plant a gentle kiss on her lips. When he finally pulled away again, the maniacal grin was back on his face.

"I want you."

And her world was once again dark.

Chapter Six

ASHLEY

"CAN I GET TWO SLICES OF cheese pizza, please? With extra, extra sauce?" Ashley signaled to the cashier at the greasiest pizza joint in all of New York City.

"Extra, extra sauce? Coming right up!" The teenager behind the counter repeated back.

Ashley took a seat at an empty booth by the window. The pizza shop was usually empty on

Friday nights; clubs and bars usually took precedent during this time, with beer-filled stomachs seeking out the greasy, fatty stuff much, much later.

But that scene was never really for her. Her partying days were more isolated to when she was in college, hopping from frat party to frat party, but truth was, she was getting too old to deal with that sort of thing nowadays. Curling up at home by the fire with a man's arms wrapped around her was a much more ideal Friday night for her. Too bad her luck with men had been pretty shitty lately.

Ashley sighed as she took a long sip of her coke. Why was it that all the men she wanted never wanted her back? The ones who did were usually the creeps she'd only go out with out of pity. Tara was the beautiful one among the two, with gorgeous blonde hair, a blemish-free face, and eyes so mesmerizing that any man would fall to their knees instantly upon looking at her.

It was too bad that her relationship with Rowan didn't work out. When she was at their wedding, everyone, including their friends and family, thought they were perfect for each other, the quintessential couple to look up to. And now when even the most compatible of relationships was falling apart, what hope was there really left for her and the other lonely hearts in the world?

"Your pizza, ma'am?"

The teenager distracted her when he placed a tray down on the table in front of her, each of the two paper plates carrying an extra-large slice of the cheesiest and sauciest pizza she could ever ask for. Even the smell alone made her want to order a whole pie just to chow down later on in shame.

She took a bite and could feel her worries all wash away. Ashley used to have a problem with food. In fact, it never really went away. She'd lived a life of isolation, always the weird loner no one wanted to hang out with, not even her parents.

Before Tara, she'd only really had one close friend, Milly, who was equally as weird as her, and they both hated the rest of the world together. It was probably the best friendship of her life, until Milly's family decided to move to Canada one day and took it all away from her. Even Tara never really measured up to Milly, caring more about her appearance and self-respect than she did about just enjoying life. Always stuck in the mud, that Tara was.

When she finished her pizzas two hours later, she looked down at her phone. Still nothing from Tara. She must've really hit it off with Declan.

Another hour passed, and still no messages came through.

"That's weird," Ashley said to herself. "She said she'd say something if she were leaving. Maybe she's still there."

She wiped the oil from her face with a paper napkin, slid out of the booth, and headed back next door. The club was due to close in just under an hour, and the place was starting to clear out. She pushed through the drunk crowd lingering by the door and walked past the tired waitresses praying to call it a night, but her friend was nowhere to be seen. Not even the obnoxiously bright emerald earrings she was wearing was enough to distinguish her from the crowd.

She walked up to the bartender and sat down.

"Excuse me, but ha—" she started to speak.

"Bar's closing soon, but what can I get for you, little lady?"

"Uh… just some water is fine. You wouldn't happen to have seen a blonde girl, would you? Long hair, green earrings, around my height?"

He shook his head as he handed her the glass. "Plenty of girls like that trickled around here tonight. Even if I had, sure as hell can't remember."

"Hey, man, can I get a vodka soda, please?" A woman around her age sat beside her while she gestured to the bartender, who shot her a thumbs up and turned away. She had a pale face, her hair styled in a short black pixie cut with hot pink highlights, and a shiny nose ring pierced in between her nostrils. She looked like she had just gotten high in one of the restroom stalls, and Ashley prayed she wouldn't try and talk to her.

"Sup," she suddenly said and turned to Ashley.

She didn't respond. She didn't want to be bothered. She just wanted to find her friend and get the hell out of here.

"Got a stick up your butt or something?" the woman said again.

Ashley shook her head. "Nothing, just looking for my friend, is all."

"Oh, yeah? Maybe I can help. I come here way, way too often. I know every face that crosses my path."

"I think I'm alright, thanks." Ashley turned her head away and resumed back to her phone, waiting for Tara's message to come through.

"You don't like me, do you? I can tell. You're all the same. You think I'm some low-life druggie who's up to nothing but trouble. Trust me, honey, no one's trying to steal your Gucci knockoff."

Ashley turned back around. She knew she wasn't being fair. The woman was just trying to start a conversation; she didn't deserve a cold shoulder. "Sorry," she mumbled. "It's nothing against you. I'm just trying to find my friend so we can go home."

"Eh, no worries. I get it all the time. Tell me about her… him… whoever." The woman whipped back her head and took another gulp of her vodka soda. "I'm Debbie, by the way. But you can call me Deb."

"Hey, Deb. I'm Ashley. And my friend's name is Tara. She's—"

"Tall, blonde, gorgeous face, and rocking body?" Deb finished for her.

Ashley nodded. "Yeah… how'd you know? You've seen her?"

"Some chick named Tara was mumbling to herself in the girl's restroom earlier tonight. Said she's meeting a Declan. Told her not to, man. Told her not to. I thought she was smart enough to turn around and leave, but given how you're here, I'm gonna go on a whim and say she went off with him. Stupid, stupid girl." She took another sip of her drink.

"What's wrong with Declan? Why should she stay away from him?"

"None of my business, man. Tried to warn them, tried to warn them all, but they're all either too stupid or too lovesick to listen to me. I'm getting too old for this shit."

"Deb!"

"What, dude? Mellow out. What's your problem?"

"My problem is that you know something about this Declan dude, and I need you to tell me what the hell is going on before my best friend gets hurt!"

She's his sister, Ashley had found out. And Declan had been a patient at Carlisle Psychiatric, a mental hospital reserved for the most troubled souls. Turned out, he wasn't new to this game. He'd been down this path before, with other girls, stalked them, lured them, seduced them, trapped them. He wasn't well, a psychological disorder of some sort. And not only that, he was dangerous, far more dangerous than Ashley could ever expect. If she wanted to see both Tara and herself alive, she couldn't go after this man alone. She needed Deb, and she needed the cops.

Deb promised she'd take Ashley over to Declan's apartment in the morning.

"But what if he kills her before then?!" Ashley screamed.

"Don't worry, he won't. I know my brother. He likes to take this… um… slow. Besides, you really think I'm gonna let the cops see me when I'm high as a kite? My mother would turn over in her grave if she knew both her fucked-up kids are in prison."

After Ashley called Deb a cab to take her home to sober up, she began to make her way back to her own apartment. She'd expected to come home with Tara, change into their pajamas, and watch scary movies all night. Now, she'd be lucky if she could even sleep. And she couldn't just run off to the cops. She'd promised Deb. She's her last hope if she wanted to find her friend.

Her mind spiraled with confusion on what to do. She couldn't just climb into bed and pretend like everything's okay, especially not when someone she cared about was potentially getting hurt.

As Ashley stepped into her apartment, she kicked her shoes off and slouched on the couch. Tara's sunflower pillow was sitting beside her, staring at her, mocking her, like she was an evil friend for just sitting here.

"Don't look at me like that," Ashley muttered, turning the pillow over. "I did what I could." She threw her hands in the air. "I need some fresh air."

She quick ran into her closet to change out of her insanely-tight dress, threw a cozy sweater and some leggings on, and headed back out the door. For the city that never sleeps, a lot of places seemed to close awfully early as she strolled toward Central Park. The night was unusually quiet, the wind was breezy, and despite the occasional honks and gunfire, New York City was as normal as it usually got.

"Here, little birdy!" She whistled as she walked down to the pond.

The night was getting chillier with each step, and she knew she had to turn around soon before things got too dangerous… and she didn't mean the cold. But when she reached the bottom step, she found out that she wasn't alone. She didn't expect anyone else to be here, especially not on a Friday night, but guess she wasn't the only one with the same idea.

"Sorry, I didn't know anyone else was down here," she muttered shyly as she turned around to walk back up the stairs.

"Ashley?" The person called out, a male voice. "Ashley, is that you?"

Ashley turned around, inching her pepper spray out from her pocket and ready to attack, when she came face-to-face with none other than the man of her dreams, Mark Roth.

"Ashley!" Mark said again as he walked closer to her. "I thought that was you. You go to my gym. I see you in my spin class every week. How's it going?"

"Hey, Mark." Ashley's face blushed red, and she turned her head away. "Not much, I guess. Just needed some air."

"Yeah, I feel you. There's a bench over there." He pointed over to their right. "Come sit down with me. Let's talk."

Ashley's body shivered when Mark took her hand. She'd always dreamt about this moment, but that was it. Just a dream. She didn't think he would ever be here with her, touching her, holding her hand. She remained speechless when he led her over to the bench. The crusty leaves and sprinkling of snow weren't enough to bother either of them. And when she sat down, she made sure to keep her distance. She didn't want him to think she was too eager to be there.

"So, what's up?" he asked.

Ashley looked at him with a confused look. "What do you mean?"

He chuckled. "I mean, it's past midnight. Usually, girls don't wander around this area during this time of the night. You know, because of the sketchy-ass homeless people."

"Yeah." She shrugged. "I guess. I just had a lot going on tonight, and I needed to be somewhere other than home to clear my head. Sorry if I'm coming across as aloof and a bitch."

Mark let out a loud laugh. "You? A bitch? Trust me, I've seen much, much worse." When his chuckles finally calmed down, he placed a hand over Ashley's again. "Wanna talk about it?"

"I don't know, not really. I don't wanna bring you down or anything."

"Ashley, I'm not sure if you know this, but I'm a licensed psychologist. I do shit like this every day, even when I don't want to. But right now, with you, I do. Now, what's bothering you? I'm all ears."

He leaned back against the bench, his arms stretched out on both sides, and waited for her to initiate the conversation.

"It's Tara," she began. "My friend. She's out with this guy who's apparently no good for her, and if I don't find her soon, she may end up d-d-dead." Ashley broke down in tears at those last words, her eyes watering and her makeup running, but she couldn't suck it all back in, despite how hard she tried.

Mark wrapped his arms around her and pulled her close to him, rubbing up and down her back as he caressed her shoulders and smoothed out her hair. "Hey, hey, hey, it's okay. Everything's going to be okay, I promise."

Ashley continued to sniffle, trying her hardest to control herself to avoid looking like a slobbering mess in front of the god himself.

"How do you know for sure?" she asked, her voice trembling and her nose running, as she pulled slightly away, his arms still wrapped around the small of her back.

"Because," he replied. "Things always seem to work out in our favor, even if it doesn't seem like it at first." He reached into his back pocket and pulled out a handkerchief, handing the plaid print over to her. "Here." He smiled.

She took it from him and smiled back. "Thanks."

"You know, Ashley, now's probably, most definitely, not the right time for this, but there's something I've been meaning to ask you for quite some time now." He rubbed the back of his neck and wiped his hands on his jeans.

She blew her nose, the sound echoing in the park and scaring away the pigeons that were pecking on scraps from several days ago.

"What's that?"

Mark shook his head and turned slightly away. "Nah, forget it, it's really bad timing. Forget I said anything."

"Hey, Mark," she whispered, placing a hand on his arm. "It's okay, you can say it. Besides, I need a good distraction. There's nothing I can really do until tomorrow morning anyway."

He rubbed the back of his neck again. "Well, I've been meaning to ask you this for weeks now, but I never really found the courage to do so."

"Is everything okay?"

He nodded. "Oh, yeah, everything's great! Well, not great, actually, given your situation." He shook his head. "I'm dancing around this again. I'm just gonna come out and say it. Ashley, would you like to go out with me? You know, like, on a date?" His face blushed red as he spoke those words, and he quickly turned away. "Sorry, that was dumb, you can say no."

"Mark," she giggled. "You're silly. And since we're being honest here, I have a confession, too. I have a massive crush on you, ever since I first joined the gym and saw you there, glistening in your sweat. Ew, why'd I just say that?"

He laughed, his voice warm. "Really? I could say the same when I first saw you."

They both burst into laughter, amused by the coincidence they found themselves in, before they both fell silent again.

"So, how about that date?" he asked again, leaning down and giving her a kiss on the cheek.

Chapter Seven
DECLAN

"GET UP! IT'S TIME FOR VITALS!" Declan Hayes shot out of bed at the sound of the echoing voice.

His hospital gown and thin mattress were nothing compared to the cushy bachelor life he had back home. Seven years ago, after the lost of his love, Serena, Declan found himself back in another psychiatric hospital, the third time that year. How many times in his entire lifetime, it was too much to count. His nonstop week of drunken self-destruction and overdosing on injections of any kind landed him back at Carlisle Psychiatric, a place he had spent more time in than any home he's ever lived in.

His mother was a violent alcoholic, and he never really found out who his father was. One simple ask always landed in him being thrown down the stairs, a punishment for his curiosity. Day after day, he saw his mother get pushed around by the men who came into her life, treating her like she was their property, following her even as she told them to leave her alone. Even restraining orders never did the trick. They all still managed to find their way back to her.

When he was fourteen, she died from an overdose, and he was forced to live on the streets, taking up odd jobs here and there to sustain a decent lifestyle. But he didn't care. Hell, he hadn't cared about anything since his mother beat it out of him when he was just six.

Declan dragged himself out of bed, IV drip still attached to his arm, and slowly waltzed over to the nurses' station.

"Number, please," the nurse at the window demanded.

"Patient 2654," he said, almost automatically.

"One sec."

When she returned five minutes later, she handed him a paper cup filled with ten different medications. "Don't forget to take the blue one. It's your mood stabilizer. We don't want a repeat of what happened last time."

Declan rolled his eyes at her, took the cup, and walked toward the dining area where everyone was eating breakfast. He took his seat in front of a gray tray, a bowl of dried oats on one side, a miniscule cup of orange juice on the other, and an almost-rotting apple laid dead and sad in the middle.

He picked around at his oats as the fat guard sitting by the door watched. Carlisle wasn't exactly known for its friendly and well-mannered patients. Once a week, at least one person tried to make a run for it, fed up with the abuse the overworked staff was serving, and attempted to bolt out the door. Great efforts, but none of them ever made it.

If they weren't caught by the fat man in time, the armed guards outside had no problem gunning them down. It wasn't a risk Declan was willing to take, especially since he knew that as long as he behaved, he'd be out in no time.

He looked down at his tiny paper cup and swirled his finger through the pills. The blue one. The menacing blue one. It was a thorn to his brain, a rock in his throat. He hated taking it. He refused!

Looking around to make sure no one was looking, he pulled open the capsule and poured the powder onto the tiled ground before hiding the rest under his tray. It was as clever as it was deadly.

Merely hours later, his mind began to change. His face twitched, his body jerked, and the piercing headache felt like a dozen bullets thrusting through his brain. He screamed, his arms flailing as he injured several other patients during group therapy. He didn't know what he was experiencing, his vision blurred with red stains. He felt like he was going to hurl, followed by a slow and painful death. And before he could find out what was really going on, he heard a cry, followed by screams of help.

He had killed someone, he found out several days later. Stabbed someone straight in the heart with a piece of the gray tray itself.

"No! I didn't do it!" When his alarm rang, Declan sprung up from his couch.

He looked around his surroundings. Back to the present day. It was all just a nightmare.

The nerves turned into a smile when he remembered the beautiful Tara Bardot still in his bedroom. He still remembered the day he found her, the beautiful goddess. It was four years ago, and she was one of the first people to sign up for the new social platform, Winks. And because she was, it didn't take long before she blew up, her content channeling in more and more views, and her face plastered all over the Internet as the hottest new influencer in New York City. Everyone knew her, and everyone loved her.

Declan was never much of an extrovert. Sure, he had a lot of luck when it came to women, but they were the ones usually drawn to him, not the other way around. And he definitely never understood the hype of Internet socialization, or any socialization for that matter. But when he turned on the news one day and saw her face, her beautiful goddess-like face that instantly drew him to her, he struggled to look away. They say love at first sight doesn't exist, but whoever said that dumb quote had never been inside Declan's mind. And he wanted her.

And because of that, he created an account and dove into the world of social media. For months, he tried mass liking her videos, commenting wherever he could, and even tried direct messaging her, all with no luck. She never noticed him, never responded to anything he sent. Even though she had several million followers, she still should've noticed him, picked him out from among the crowd as her number one fan, and paid attention to him. And when she didn't do that, he got angry. He had spent all this time not only creating an account, but also day after day following her, and she still refused to give him the time of day.

He almost gave up hope. Year after year spent wallowing in self-loathing and depression, yearning for the woman he believed was his soulmate. He became suicidal, almost at his breaking point, a knife held to his wrist and reminding him of the person he used to hate, when a miracle happened. She messaged him. She wanted him.

"Don't you think you should, you know, stabilize yourself first before you jump into something like this? Someone could get seriously hurt." He was sitting on a park bench by Central Park with his sister, Debbie, the night of his date.

He'd been so ecstatic that he finally got a chance to be with the love of his life that his sister was the only person he knew of to tell. But like all older sisters, she disapproved.

"I mean, you JUST got out of the hospital. If Mom were here—"

"Well, she's not, okay?" he raised his voice and yelled. "She's dead, just like she should be. She was nothing but a deadbeat. What makes you think I care whether she approves or not?"

Debbie could only shake her head. She didn't understand. She just didn't understand. She had a different life. She got to live with their grandparents while he was stuck with their alcoholic mother. She didn't know what he was going through, what it meant for him to finally be able to have something he so desperately wanted for so long.

A thud was heard in the next room over. He threw the pillow off of him and stood up, the empty beer bottle that was on him tumbling down and rolling across the floor. When he walked into the room, there she was, as beautiful and magnificent as she was when he first saw her. Her skin looked so smooth. Her blonde hair so silky as the strands draped down her back.

She was so radiant, the aura around her gesturing him to come closer.

"Come here, Declan. I'm all yours, remember? Show me how you really feel about me."

Declan nodded, his pants tightening, and his palms sweaty. He clenched his fists together and made his way over to the woman, his soulmate. An arm reached out from Tara and caressed the side of his face, slithering down toward his body and massaging his chest.

"I'm all yours," she whispered before leaning up to kiss him on the lips.

Am I hallucinating? Declan thought to himself.

His mind was rushing, and his vision continued to fade in and out, but nothing was strong enough to take him away from this passionate affair. Pulling a key out from his back pocket, he unlocked her cuffs, picked her up by the waist, and carried her to bed. He then undressed himself and climbed on top of her, dancing his bare body over hers and caressing her perfect breasts with his lips. She moaned in his ear as he went down on her, inserting himself inside her when he came back up. He moaned back as she nibbled on his ears and whispered sweet words of passion. He couldn't help but fall victim to the sensual woman below him, and within mere moments, he finished.

When he woke up several hours later, she was gone.

Chapter Eight
TARA

"INFLUENCER, MY ASS," Tara scoffed as she continued to wrestle her wrists free from the confines of the cuffs.

But it was no use. The more she pulled, the tighter the grip seemed to get, and she found herself worse off than she had been before.

She reflected back to her life, just a few days ago. How naïve she'd been when she stupidly agreed to sign up for that dumb app. She knew she should've just stuck with her solemn stalking of her ex-husband, a hopeless romantic from afar, but Ashley just had to be so convincing, telling her to get a life. And look where that got her.

What happened to her? She used to have it all, and not because of her fame on social media. She used to be someone, a beauty queen, America's sweetheart, the girl all the boys loved and all the girls wanted to be. She didn't care about hooking up or fame. She didn't care about what people thought of her or whether someone judged her. She had a mind of her own. She was smart. And that's why Rowan fell in love with her.

But somewhere down the line, it just all vanished. She became more self-obsessed, more focused on strangers on the Internet than on her own husband. She became obsessed with wanting to be someone, with wanting to be seen, that she never stopped to realize how dangerous that could actually be. Maybe, just maybe, if she had remained a nobody, Declan would've never found her, and she wouldn't be finding herself trapped in a man's bedroom right now.

"I swear, if I ever get out of this, I'm swearing off men forever."

The hunger pangs were really starting to kick in now, and she felt herself growing lightheaded. She stared down at the bowl of oats Declan had left for her, as dry and unappetizing as her attraction toward him. She couldn't eat his food. If she did, she'd be reinforcing her dependence on him, and it'd be much harder to escape.

Tara still couldn't understand how someone so handsome, so gorgeous, could turn out to be such a monster. What had hurt him in his past? Whatever it was, she didn't have time to wait for him to tell her. She could be dead by then. There was only one way, only one way he'd let her go. The same way all men lost their inhibitions around a pretty face.

She kicked hard against the bed frame to catch his attention, using everything she had to force a smile on her lips. Minutes later, he walked in, just as she had expected. He still had on his oil-stained sweats and ripped T-shirt, his hair greasy, and his face beginning to break out. But still, beneath all the stains and dirt, he was still as handsome as handsome could get, and a part of her still wished he hadn't turned out to be such a sociopath.

"Come here, Declan. I'm all yours, remember? Show me how you really feel about me." As she spoke, she almost believed her words. The look on his face was so innocent, so vulnerable, just like it had been on that first night.

Declan nodded, his pants tightening, and his palms sweaty. He clenched his fists together and made his way over to Tara as she winced, unsure of whether he was able to see right through her. Tara reached an arm out and caressed the side of his face, slithering down toward his body and massaging his chest.

"I'm all yours," she whispered before leaning up to kiss him on the lips.

She could feel his entire body shaking, like he wasn't expecting such a change in behavior from his captive. And she didn't blame him. It *was* odd that someone would go from being so cold and rash to engaging in the art of seduction.

She watched with anxiousness when she saw him slowly pull a key from out his back pocket, uncuffed her, picked her up by the waist, and carried her to bed. She could've tried to fight, bite him, scratch him, kick him as hard as she could, anything to get away. But given the size of his muscles and his protruding veins, she knew there was a slim chance she'd be able to escape far.

It also didn't help that the size of his girth when he undressed himself made her swoon with lust. If he'd just been any other guy, the guy she thought she was meeting on that seemingly innocent app, she would've thought she'd have a chance at a relationship with him. The daily rituals of sex surely would've been a blessing.

As he climbed on top of her, dancing his bare body over hers and caressing her breasts with his lips and tongue, she moaned. His hands were so gentle and smooth, and they knew the exact places they had to be on her, starting from her chest down to her hips, and soon, she found his mouth in between her thighs. It wasn't supposed to be so easy, so simple, but as he continued to explore her body, her anger toward him seemed to fade away.

And when he inserted himself inside her, she felt as though she'd found the missing piece of her puzzle, their bodies intertwined so well that she almost found herself falling in love with him. Almost. He moaned back as she nibbled on his ears and whispered sweet words of passion, driving him to the brink of ecstasy before he finished mere seconds later.

When Tara woke up an hour later, she found his arm draped around her bare breasts like a blanket. Her head was still spinning, and she wanted nothing more than to just lie back down and cuddle beside him.

"No!" she whispered loudly to herself, suddenly remembering where she was.

She looked down at her wrists. They were free. She looked down at her ankles. Nothing around them, either. Now was her chance. She carefully lifted his arm off from her body and slid over the side to roll off. She then quickly threw on the first T-shirt she could find, his, and tiptoed toward the door. But when she got there, she stopped, turned her head, and looked back at the man sleeping soundly in bed. She didn't know why, but the guilt of betraying him began to build up inside her, and she almost felt like she was committing a crime by leaving.

But when she looked down at the cuts and bruises on her wrists from when she tried to break free from his confines, her senses began coming back. She was his captive. And he was clearly psychologically insane. It was crazy to think that anything more than a death sentence could come out of this relationship.

When she finally got to the front door, she looked back and paused once again, almost stepping back inside, when she heard a loud thump on the wall, followed by Declan, charging at her like a raging bull. She slammed the door shut behind her and started to run. He was much taller and much faster than her, and her heart pounded harder and harder in her chest, afraid for her life and regretting having looked back. She bolted down the cul-de-sac and turned the nearest corner, her eyes focused on the woods in front of her. If she could make it there, maybe she'd be able to hide behind some trees to lose him.

But before she could, she bumped into a familiar face. Deb. The girl from the club. The girl who warned Tara about Declan.

"You!" Tara exclaimed.

"Hey, you're that girl. I know you. Fancy running into you here."

Tara had so many questions, so many explanations, so many things she wanted to say, but when the growls behind her came closer, none of that mattered anymore.

"Run! He's coming! Run!" she screamed, trying to pull loose from Debbie's grip. "What are you doing? Let me go! Let me go!"

"Declan, stop!" Debbie said sternly as he approached closer to them.

"This doesn't concern you, Deb. Now, step aside."

"No, you're not taking her, not again." Her voice suddenly lowered. "Really, Declan? Haven't you learned your lesson from the last one? What's her name, Val?"

"Vicky," he corrected her.

"Right, her."

"How… how do you two know each other?" Tara asked, her body still trembling and trying to pull away from Debbie, but her grip was even stronger than Declan's.

"He's my brother," she said, an answer that surprised her. "And a shitty one at that."

"Give me the girl, Deb," Declan repeated. "Give me the girl, and no one gets hurt."

But Debbie shook her head. "Still as stubborn as ever. You really haven't learned anything from Mom—"

"Mom's DEAD!" Declan's face grew bright red, and he charged at Debbie.

Tara winced and closed her eyes, preparing for the blow that would soon occur, but instead, she heard a gun fire, followed by a loud thud on the ground.

When she opened her eyes again, Declan's body was lying on the ground, with two cops standing behind him.

"H-How'd—"

"I called the cops," Debbie said, as if reading her mind. "When your friend Ashley came into the club looking for you, I sensed that you'd gone off. He probably drugged you, took you home in a taxi, seduced you. He does it with all the girls. It's his ritual."

"Oh my god! Tara! You're alive!"

Tara heard a female voice scream her name, and when she looked up, she saw Ashley running toward her. She didn't care that her hair was a tangled mess, and she was wearing nothing but a pizza-stained T-shirt. She couldn't be happier to see her friend after all this time. She thought she'd die in Declan's apartment, and no one would even notice.

With her arms wrapped around Ashley, Tara couldn't help but look over at Declan and the cops. They had him cuffed and restrained, shoving him into one of their cars, head first, before driving away. She knew she should've felt a sense of relief, a feeling of safety that the monster was going to now be locked up.

So, why didn't she?

One Night Stand

Chapter Nine
ROWAN

"ROWAN, HONEY," FAITH SAID, walking over to him. "Is everything okay with you? Your mind seems to be elsewhere lately."

Rowan was lounging on the couch, one leg slung over onto the cushion while a beer rested in his right hand.

"Huh?" He looked up at her, and for a moment, Tara's face crossed his mind. But when he blinked again, Faith came back into his vision. "Oh, nothing. I'm fine."

"You don't seem fine." She sat down on the couch beside him, rubbing his leg with her hand, but he quickly pulled it away. "What's going on with you?"

"I said, nothing!" He turned off the TV, chugged the rest of his beer, and stood up. "I'm going for a walk."

"But it's almost midnight! Where are you going?"

"Just... just out, okay? Get off my back. I need some air."

Rowan roughly grabbed his coat and threw a scarf over his face before slipping his shoes on. The red and yellow scarf brought back many memories, taking his mind back to the time when Tara had knitted it for him for their one-year anniversary. Neither of them had much, but he'd treasured this scarf ever since. Of course, Faith never found out about it. That the one piece of item he could never seem to part with was the one given to him by his ex-wife.

Rowan managed to make it down several streets before stopping into a nearby bar. The streets of Boston were much calmer than those of New York City. Colder, sure, but he'd take the drop in temperature over the increase in crime any day.

He'd never told her, but Faith had always been his rebound. He thought moving all the way to Boston and starting a new life with a new woman would distract him from Tara and make him see that he was much better without her. And it was fun at first, great, actually. Faith treated him the way Tara used to, always showed up on time, and never let herself fall victim to social media. It was everything he'd wanted that Tara couldn't give him. But there was just one problem. She wasn't Tara. And though he thought Faith was capable of replacing her, she just couldn't, and Rowan had resented Faith ever since he moved up here with her.

"Can I get a lager, please?" he gestured to the bartender when he walked inside.

Perth's Pub was never usually crowded, not even on weekends, and because of that, it remained one of his favorite places to grab a drink. He hated large crowds, the smells, the loud noises, the puke, no, he wasn't for any of it.

"Rough night?" the man asked when he set down his beer on top of a thin coaster.

"Woman problems."

"Ah, I know the feeling. Wife ran off with my kids just last week. Haven't heard from them since."

That got his attention. "Really? Why? You didn't try looking for them?"

Pat, his name tag said. He gave Rowan a long sigh. "Oh, trust me, I've tried. Woman just woke up one day and told me she didn't love me anymore, and just like that, she was gone. Besides, there's not much I can do anyway. They were her kids; I just happened to have bonded with them."

"I'm sorry, man, that sucks."

Pat shrugged. "Nothing you can really do when life kicks you in the face like that. You just gotta get back up and continuing living. But if an old man like me were to give anyone advice, it'll be this. When you love a woman, don't let her go, even if you think there's someone better out there. Trust me, there isn't. If I could go back to the woman I had fifteen years ago, maybe I wouldn't be living out of a studio apartment right now."

"Thanks, I'll keep that in mind." Rowan checked his watch. "Listen, man, I gotta run, but I hope everything gets better for you."

"Yeah, yeah, I'll be fine." Pat waved. "Just don't fuck up your own life.

Rowan ran through the door to his and Faith's shared apartment and pulled out his suitcase. He then ran over to his dresser and started stacking his clothes into it.

"Rowan?" Faith was half asleep when she turned on the lights and saw her boyfriend on the floor of their room. "What are you doing?"

Without even looking up, he answered, "I'm sorry, Faith, but I can't do this anymore. I have to leave."

"Leave? Are you going to your parents? When are you coming back?"

"I'm not, Faith, I'm not. I'm going back to New York, and I'm not coming back." He stood up and walked over to her, plopping himself onto the bed beside her. "I'm sorry, Faith. I should've told you sooner, but I don't think this is going to work out. We're… we're just not good for each other."

Faith crossed her arms over her chest. "It's Tara, isn't it? You're going back to her, after you promised me that you were completely and utterly over her. Now, you're going back?! Why would you do this to me, Rowan? Why? I introduced you to my parents. I told them about our future together. And now you're leaving?"

"Why the hell would you do that? We never discussed a future together. I didn't think meeting your parents meant we had to get married."

"But we're so good together! You even said it yourself! Tara was a bitch!"

Rowan raised a fist as Faith winced back. He then caught himself and lowered it back down. "I'm sorry, Faith. I didn't plan this, but I have to go. I'm sorry."

Without another word shared between them, he picked up his suitcase, grabbed his coat and scarf, and hopped into his car, driving south and refusing to stop until he reached the New York City interstate.

"DUDE, YOU REALLY GOTTA STOP obsessing."

When Rowan got back to the city, he hit up friend after friend, trying to find someone who would let him crash with them while he looked for a job and a new apartment.

Unfortunately, he'd burned most of his bridges when he decided to say "adios" to almost everyone he knew before leaving. To the ones he didn't, an Irish goodbye was enough to do the trick. Luckily, his childhood friend, Alex Winters, agreed to put up with him for a few weeks, forcing Rowan to promise that he'd get his life together and never bail again.

"I'm not obsessing, Alex. I'm just checking up on her."

Alex walked over to where Rowan was sitting and snatched the phone out of his hands. "You're obsessing."

"Yo, dude, give that back!" He managed to wrestle his phone out from Alex's grasp and scrolled back to the page he was on. "I don't understand. Where is it?"

"Where's what?" Rowan could tell that Alex was rolling his eyes at him; the glare he shot over at him was difficult to ignore.

"Her page! Her Winks page. It's gone!"

"Maybe you have the wrong handle."

"No, I have it memorized like the back of my hand."

"Maybe it's set on private."

"No, she'd never do that. She has too many fans relying on her."

"Dude! I don't know! Maybe she deleted it. Or maybe she blocked you!" Alex crossed his arms over his chest. "Besides, you're the one who left her. Maybe it's a taste of your own karma."

Rowan was shocked by his comment. He'd never really thought about it like that. Six years, Tara and him had been married, dating ever since they first met in high school. She was just always... there, whenever he needed her. And he'd always taken her for granted. Even when they'd fight, Tara had been there, bringing him back to his senses. Maybe Alex was right.

"Maybe she did block me," he said quietly, his head lowered.

"Yeah, probably. Sorry for being a douche, man. But all I'm saying is, if someone who vowed to love me forever decided to dump me and shack up in another state with someone else, I'd be pretty pissed off, too. If you want her back, really want her back and not just because you're horny, don't stalk her. Give her some time; she'll reach out to you if it's meant to be." Alex looked down at his watch. "Shit, I'm late for work." He reached over the counter and grabbed his keys and wallet. "Just give it time, dude. She'll come around."

"Right," Rowan replied, his voice hesitant that his relationship with Tara would ever return back to normal.

Chapter Ten
TARA

TWO MONTHS LATER, TARA found herself sitting on a park bench and sipping on a cup of hot cocoa on a chilly winter day. A lot had changed since her time at Declan's. She'd tried returning back to her usual life, her streams, and her life on the Internet, but every time she turned on her camera, she felt terrified that Declan was watching her. From somewhere. From anywhere. From prison. Or if not him, someone else. She couldn't handle being in the limelight, exposed to potential criminals on the Internet, and eventually, her paranoia forced her to shut down her account… permanently.

"Tara?"

She looked up, a thin layer of cocoa mustache on her upper lip, and saw Rowan. He had his hands stuffed in the pockets of his coat, the tip of his nose was red from the cold, and wrapped around his neck was the red and yellow scarf she had knitted for him on their one-year anniversary.

Tara smiled. She had almost forgotten about Rowan. Though it had only been a few months, it felt like years had gone by since she was last with Rowan, since she had last obsessed over Rowan. Maybe her experience with Declan had taught her a lesson, and it took dancing a tango with death to finally break her out of her delusion.

"Hi, Rowan," she replied, taking another sip of her cocoa.

She wasn't expecting it when he sat down beside her, crossing one leg over the other and resting an arm behind her.

"What's going on with you?" he asked as he sighed.

She raised a brow at him. "What do you mean?"

"You haven't been online lately. Your channel, your feed, all gone. I was getting concerned."

Tara shrugged. "I decided that it wasn't for me anymore. It's too much, you know? Keeping up with the constant crowd was way more than I could handle."

Rowan chuckled.

"What?"

"Well, Tara, I could've told you that." He chuckled again.

"Oh, stop." She gave him a playful tap on the arm, but then remembered what he had said. "Wait, you were concerned about me?"

"Of course, Tara. You really think I stopped thinking about you? Never!"

"Well… yeah, kind of. I thought you were with what's her face, Hope, Joy—"

"Faith," he corrected her. "Nah, that was just a little fling. Things fizzled out pretty quickly. Moved back into town just a couple days ago. In all honesty, Tara, I was hoping I'd run into you. No one could ever really replace you."

She didn't know what to say. She'd wanted this. For weeks after he left her, she'd wanted nothing more than to have him back, to hold him, to be with him, and now that he was here, she didn't quite feel the same as she did before.

"Yeah, that's what I thought about you when you left."

"Really?" Rowan turned his body to face her, his cold breath releasing from his mouth every few seconds. "Wow, and here I was thinking you'd gone on to find someone better." He reached out and grabbed her by the hands. "What do you say, Tara? What do you say we give this another chance? No Faith, no other guy, no Internet, just you and me."

Tara didn't know how to respond. She knew it made sense for her and Rowan to be together; it always made sense, from being high school sweethearts to being the first of their friends to have ever gotten married. It just made sense. But when he touched her hands, it just didn't feel right, like there was someone else out there who was better for her, whom she felt more connected to, and she knew she'd be doing her heart a great injustice.

She pulled her hands away and stood up. "I'm sorry, Rowan. I love you, and I'll always love you, but I can't. My heart belongs to someone else."

As she walked away, she expected Rowan to chase after her, to grab her by the shoulders and plant a passionate kiss on her, telling her that she's his world, and that he'd do anything, literally anything, to be with her. But he didn't. He simply walked away in the opposite direction, thus solidifying her decision.

Tara didn't know what she was thinking as she made her way home. She wasn't really sure where her mind was at, but she knew where she needed it to be.

Her new apartment studio was located on the south side of Brooklyn. It wasn't much, but it was enough to get by until she was able to find a job that required more skill than just a pretty face. She still met up with Ashley once in a while. She'd given up on her plan of going to San Francisco, finding a job nearby instead so she could stay close to her family and loved ones. But the tension between them grew when Ashley started dating Mark, who wasn't so fond of their lack of privacy. It was for the best, anyway. That way, she wouldn't be able to find out what Tara was up to.

She walked into her closet and changed into her red sequin dress before throwing her winter coat back over it, and she was back out the door. A forty-minute train ride later, she found herself standing outside of New York City's correctional facility. She knew the drill. Show her ID, sign in, and wait.

"Hi, Declan," she said with a smile when she saw him walking over to her, cuffs and chains around his wrists and ankles.

He smiled back at her. "I didn't think I'd ever see you again."

"I didn't think so, either," she giggled. "But there's just something in my heart that tells me this is where I belong, with you."

As he inched closer to her, she pulled him into a kiss.

One Night Stand

One Night Stand

One Night Stand

One Night Stand

www.ingramcontent.com/pod-product-compliance
Lightning Source LLC
Chambersburg PA
CBHW030352200726

48286CB00013B/1089

*9 7 8 1 9 5 2 7 1 6 4 3 0 *